THE HATCHING

THE

NIGHTMARE

CLUB

THE HATCHING

ANNIE GRAVES

ILLUSTRATED BY
GLENN MCELHINNEY

MINNEAPOLIS

First published in Dublin, Ireland by Little Island
Original edition © Little Island 2013

American edition © 2015 Darby Creek,
a division of Lerner Publishing Group, Inc.

Darby Creek
A division of Lerner Publishing Group, Inc.
241 First Avenue North
Minneapolis, MN 55401 USA

For reading levels and more information, look up this title
at www.lernerbooks.com.

Main body text set in ITC Stone Serif Std. 11.5/15.
Typeface provided by Adobe Systems.

Library of Congress Cataloging-in-Publication Data

Graves, Annie.
    The Hatching / by Annie Graves ; illustrated by
    Glenn McElhinney.
        pages   cm. — (The Nightmare Club)
    Originally published: Dublin, Ireland : Little Island,
2013.
    ISBN: 978–1–4677–4354–9 (lib. bdg. : alk. paper)
    ISBN: 978–1–4677–4354–9 (eBook)
    [1. Eggs—Fiction. 2. Horror stories.] I. McElhinney,
Glenn, illustrator. II. Title.
PZ7.G77512Hat 2015
[Fic]—dc23   2014015446

Manufactured in the United States of America
1 – SB – 12/31/14

*To Sally Ann,
who's scared of nothing.
My kind of girl.*

*A*nnie Graves is twelve years old, and she has no intention of ever growing up. She is, conveniently, an orphan, and lives at an undisclosed address in the Glasnevin area of Dublin, Ireland, with her pet toad, Much Misunderstood, and a small black kitten, Hugh Shalby Nameless.

You needn't think she goes to school—pah!—or has anything as dull as brothers and sisters or hobbies, but let's just say she keeps a large black cauldron on the stove.

This is not her first book. She has written eight so far, none of which is her first.

Publisher's note: we did try to take a picture of Annie, but her face just kept fading away. We have sent our camera for investigation but suspect the worst.

THANK YOU!!

Listen, Dee Sullivan, if you think you wrote this story, you are seriously deranged. You may have been eating too many eggs. But, hey, I dòn't mind admitting to a little harmless help.

A few sort of hints and mutterings.

OK?
SATISFIED?

Seamus was the next to tell a story.

If the truth be told, I don't really like Seamus.

He is the sort of boy who wouldn't actually push you into the mud on purpose, but he would run past you without looking, and you'd end up in the mud.

Even if he hadn't meant to do it, the end result would be the same. You'd have a rotten squelchy uniform for the rest of the day.

You get my drift...

Seamus cleared his throat and began
to speak.

He said his story was about an egg.

I smiled evilly. *Someone* was definitely
going home as soon as his stupid little tale
was over.

It reminded me
of Gregory, who
told a story about
waking up having
grown a mad little
tail, and how it would
wag whenever he was
happy and how annoying
that was.

*People like Gregory and Seamus don't
really get the point of the Nightmare Club*,
I thought smugly, leaning back on the
cushions and popping another gummy
bear into my mouth.

And then . . .

"The affair of the Egg began," Seamus said, "as these things always do, with a dare."

As these things always do?

Hmm.

Well, go on, read it for yourself. See what you make of it.

"Eat this," yelled Sally Ann, brandishing an egg in front of my face, "and I'll give you five dollars."

"What kind of egg is that?" I asked her.

"I don't know," she said. "I found it on the road."

1

Sally Ann was always finding things on the road.

Old keys.

Belt buckles.

Pages out of books.

Eggs were new, though. I don't think she'd ever found an egg before.

I didn't eat it.

But she thrust it at
me, and I took it
from her.

I wish she had kept it.

I wish she'd never shown
me the cursed thing.

I wish against wish that the Egg had remained on the road to be buried in muck and car dust and never noticed by anyone at all.

As soon as I touched the Egg, I felt a shiver run up the small bones in my wrist.

It was almost like the feeling I got the time I had a secret go with Mum's electric chainsaw. Only without the glee. A sort of dull shock.

I put it in my pocket all the same.

After all, it was only an egg.

I felt its smooth weight against my leg,
like a promise.

A promise of what, I did not know. I don't
speak Egg.

I forgot about it then, and it stayed
nestled in my pocket throughout the
school day.

That evening, I changed into my pajamas and the Egg remained, neglected, in my gray uniform pants pocket.

But in the night I suddenly awoke and it was there, looming whitely on my nightstand.

It wasn't a pink, grainy egg like hens lay.

It was a white, perfect one, like the kind of egg you see in picture books.

"Maybe it's a duck egg," said my mother when I went to put it in the fridge the following morning.

She denied going through my pockets and placing the Egg on my bedside table, but years of experience had taught me that she was an expert snooper. No catapult un-confiscated, no firecracker un-removed, all without ever admitting to any of it.

In a house like mine there are no secrets, but there are a lot of unspoken things. Mum never makes a fuss, just quietly fixes the problem at hand, wiping it down like the surface of a table or a countertop until you don't really remember what was there in the beginning of it all.

When I got home, the Egg was on my
nightstand again.

I returned it to the fridge and closed
the door the way Mum says I should,
pressing it tightly, so the seal inside sucks
it firmly shut.

I awoke to its eggy presence on my
nightstand yet again.

That was when I realized that I was scared
of the Egg.

This was a very embarrassing thing to realize.

Boys my age shouldn't be scared of eggs.

Especially when they're best friends with Sally Ann, who isn't scared of anything and once ate a living spider "for the laugh."

I hated the Egg for making me feel so powerless.

I sat up in bed and stared at it.

It was so still and smooth and perfect.
Mum had rinsed it under the tap, so it was
cleaner now than it had been.

It gleamed dully through the darkness,
lurking eggily.

In the morning I put it in the center of
the kitchen table.

When Mum came in, I told her what
had happened.

We don't flat-out *accuse* people of things
in my house, but the Egg itself was
accusation enough, lolling on its side like
a Roman emperor.

Mum said, "Oh, for goodness' sake," and she smashed the Egg into the sink.

We looked at each other with a sickening kind of relief: I because my enemy had been defeated, and she because, for the first time in living memory, she had wasted food.

In school that day I was giddy with relief.

I spent recess happily collecting slugs
with Sally Ann in the hopes of luring, and
eventually trapping, Flaherty the Hedgehog.

He was a mythical creature said to roam around the school garden late at night in search of food and fallen bits of lunch.

Sally Ann was obsessed with Flaherty because she was fairly sure that he didn't exist, except as a sort of schoolwide conspiracy to deny that there were rats in the yard.

These rats sometimes made their way into the school building.

If we ever actually found them, there'd have to be extra time off while the school was made child-friendly again with a mixture of traps and poison.

That is probably why they made this Flaherty fellow up.

Sally Ann is probably the cleverest person I know.

I didn't tell her about the Egg, though.

I couldn't tell anyone about the Egg. I was too ashamed.

When I got home, the Egg was on the nightstand once again, whole. Not one crack marred its perfect, eggy surface.

This time I shoved it in a drawer and didn't tell Mum.

There were a few reasons for this.

1. I WAS AFRAID OF WHAT SHE'D SAY.

2. I DIDN'T WANT TO WORRY HER.

3. I WAS GOING **MAD**.

And I *was* going mad, at least a little.

All night I stayed up, thinking about eggs and imagining little sounds coming from the drawer.

There were no sounds coming from the drawer. The Egg has never to my knowledge made a noise. I don't know if it even could.

It probably could, though. The Egg could probably do whatever the Egg wanted to do.

In the morning
it was on the
nightstand again.

Beside the lamp
with the soccer balls
all over it that Mum
had been given by a friend
whose little boy was too old for
it now.

That lamp was pretty stupid-looking, but
I pretended to like it in the hopes that I'd
get more presents.

I prefer playing hurling to soccer anyway. Mainly because in hurling you get to have a wooden stick for hitting the ball, and that's as close to a weapon as a kid my age gets, really.

The Egg was awful.

I wanted to crack it open and flush the insides down the toilet.

But at the same time, I knew it would be back. And I *really* didn't want to make it angry.

When I got home from school that evening,
it was on the edge of the nightstand.

It should have been teetering wildly, but
the Egg didn't teeter. It perched decidedly.

Mum had vacuumed my room, but when we ate dinner she didn't say anything about the Egg.

Maybe she never noticed it.

Maybe only I could see the Egg now that it had risen from the gooey dead.

That night I awoke to find the Egg
on my stomach, pressed down into it
almost roughly.

It felt heavier than it had the last time
I had picked it up.

I tried to roll it off me, but I couldn't. I tried to peel it off, but it had stuck to my skin like those bandages you get when the doctor takes your blood.

I got the lamp from my nightstand and
lifted it up above my bare stomach.

Again and again I brought it down
upon the Egg, and again and
again the Egg remained flawlessly,
heartbreakingly whole.

Eventually I gave up and cried myself to angry, dreamless sleep.

In the
morning
Mum kept
me home from
school. I was running a temperature, and
I also had an egg stuck to my abdomen.

She didn't know about that last part,
though.

I don't know why I didn't tell her.
Something inside me seemed to know
that the Egg demanded secrecy about the
process. Loyalty.

I had not been loyal when I tried to smash
it with the soccer lamp.

But I would be loyal now.

Days passed, and the doctor came to
visit and took my blood. He tried to lift
up my pajama top and check if it was
appendicitis, but I wouldn't let him.

If he saw the Egg, he would probably try
to remove the Egg, to hurt it. And the Egg
must not be hurt.

Especially at this most vulnerable of times.

You see, the Egg was beginning to hatch.

Cracks had appeared at the top of it, and eventually they snaked all the way across its body.

It didn't move, though. The Egg was a static being, still and ominous.

On the fourth day of what I had come to think of as the Hatching, the cracks began to unfurl.

They didn't move, but somehow they opened without moving.

It was like watching a series of still photographs with slight differences. The cracks were widening and widening and widening and opening and everything was swirling around me, a terrible eggy blackness reaching out and out and out.

When I awoke there was an egg on my nightstand again.

It was almost identical to the previous Egg, except that it was very slightly bigger.

Every morning I put the new Egg in the fridge, and every evening it returns to the nightstand.

I am still scared of the Egg, but there's another feeling there too.

A sort of a horrid responsibility for its well-being.

After all, I brought it into this world, in this form anyway.

I touch the new Egg sometimes, stroke
it softly round and round and round—
the whorls of my fingertips so rough
in comparison.

They really are a higher life form, eggs.
Such simple things, and yet containing
worlds. Nourishment and life.

Meat and venom.

Best to stay on their good side. Not that
eggs have sides.

But still, you know what I mean.

I was just about to open my mouth and mock Seamus when he lifted up his T-shirt.

There it was: a perfect egg-shaped dent sunk into the soft fat of his belly.

"I call it my nest," he concluded proudly, and everyone went quiet.

Until John muttered, "I'd probably still eat
it. For five dollars."

I'D LIKE TO SEE HIM TRY.

I REALLY,
REALLY
WOULD.

THE END

Check out
all the titles in

THE
Nightmare
Club

A DOG'S
BREAKFAST

ANNIE GRAVES

THE
Nightmare
Club

HELP!
MY BROTHER'S
A ZOMBIE

ANNIE GRAVES

THE
Nightmare
Club